BOOT

KAKI

STØVLE

FOOT

COKOR

HENDRIK DRESCHER

HYPERI ON BOOKS FOR CHILDREN • NEW YORK

Louise was born a **KLUTZ.**
SHE couldn't *help it,*
it was **a family** condition.

momma KLUTZ

Ever since the beginning...

WO- OPS!

WOOPS-z-z-z!

A **Klutz** popped up at the *Hindenburg* explosion.

When the *Titanic* sank, a Klutz was at the helm.

KLUTZES were BUNGLING *fools.*

The Egyptians had a Klutz. So did the STONE Age.

Like their **ancestors**,

OBSTACLE

Louise and her parents **klutzed** away their days.

Their CLUMSINESS would start AT the croak of dawn.

By LUNCHTIME they were *really* cooking.

However, to the *amazement* of their NEIGHBORS, the **KLUTZES** never got **seriously** hurt. As clumsy as they were, the **KLUTZES** were *twice* that lucky!

LUMPISH YOKELS LUMPISH YOKELS LUMPISH YOKELS

Everywhere the **KLUTZES** went,

Lumpish yokels...

LUMPFISH YODELS

YODELS

people called them *lumpish yokels.*

LUMPISH YOKELS...

CIRCUS

To AVOID their critics, they often drove through the pitch of night.

So did PROFESSOR SQUIRMWORM'S *Magic Circus caravan* on its way to the next BIG city.

One evening PopPa **Klutz** was fiddling with the radio while racing down a twisting mountain road.

WHEN **BANG!**

they met with the CIRCUS caravan.

Unhurt *as usual*, the **Klutzes** staggered out of the wreck.

Professor Squirmworm rubbed his eyes and *glared* at the threesome. The *glare* changed into a STARE. Then he cracked a big SMILE, which turned into a *full-blown, rip-roaring* belly laugh. "AT LONG LAST—THE CLOWN FAMILY I'VE BEEN LOOKING FOR!" And with that the **Klutzes** found their calling in life.

They were *magnificent* clowns.
No one had *ever* seen **such** hayseed shenanigans before.
People had to be carried out on stretchers from laughing *too* much.

One day Leonora the Lion Tamer asked Louise why she wore such **big, clunky** *boots*. Louise explained that the entire **Klutz family** for generations had been born **with them on!**

After **mulling** it over for a while Louise and Leonora decided it was time to *expose those toes*. Aside from being as STINKY as thousand-year-old cheese, Louise's feet were *tiny and very beautiful.*

No sooner had they *cooled down* from being LOCKED up since birth

than she was using *them* to dance around the **tent**.

She *danced* ALL night.

By morning she was doing *pirouettes*

and *balancing* on the tightrope.

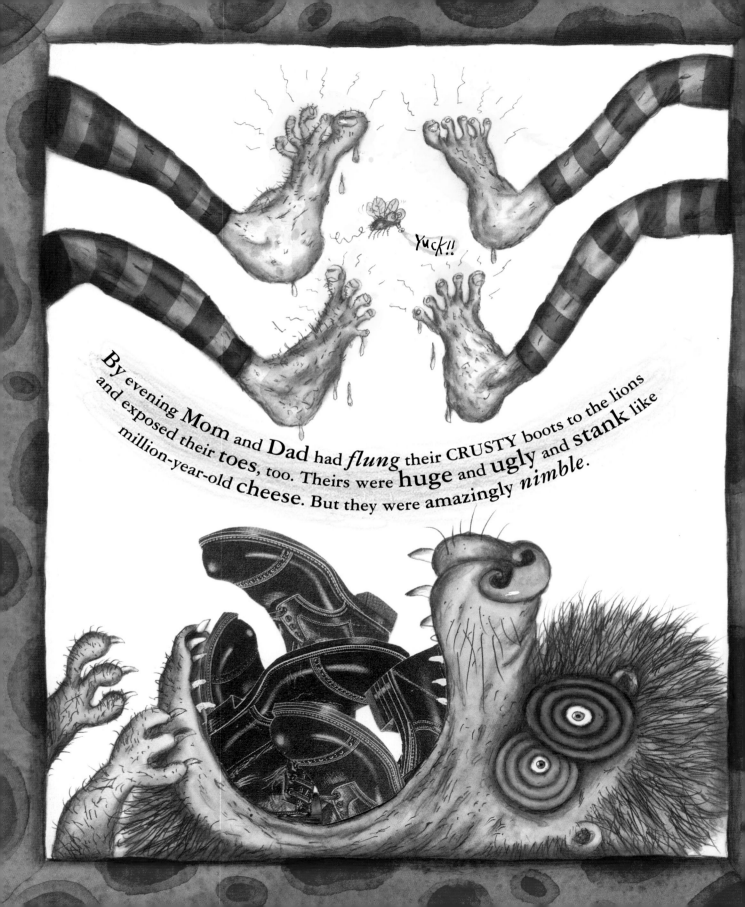

YUCK!!

By evening Mom and Dad had *flung* their CRUSTY boots to the lions and exposed their **toes**, too. Theirs were **huge** and **ugly** and **stank** like million-year-old **cheese**. But they were amazingly *nimble*.

Soon enough they were all *swinging* from the trapeze. Professor Squirmworm's mouth DROPPED open at the sight of his flying clowns.

"YOU'RE HIRED . . . AGAIN," he *yelled* up toward the tent's dome. And with that the **Klutzes** found their new true calling in life.

From that day on they were as *delicate* and *graceful* as ballerinas They performed for KINGS and PAUPERS around the globe and were *espec* which **they did** while *juggling* five eels and *whistling* "Dixie"

(ROPE THAT HOLDS THE TENT UP!)

on thin ice and came to be known as the **Magnificent Flying Klutzes**.

ially well liked for their *backward triple somersault razzmatazz flip,*

with crackers in their mouths. **Always flawlessly!**

Library of Congress Cataloging-in-Publication Data

Drescher, Henrik.

Klutz / text and illustrations by Henrik Drescher.

— 1st ed.   p.   cm.

Summary: A family with a long history of clumsiness
discovers their unexpected true calling
as nimble-footed circus performers.

ISBN 0-7868-0233-2 (trade)

ISBN 0-7868-2182-5 (lib. bdg.)

[1. Clumsiness—Fiction. 2. Circus—Fiction.] Title.

PZ7.D78383K1 1996   [E]—dc20   95-43625